Little Pear
The Story of
a Little Chinese Boy

ELEANOR FRANCES LATTIMORE

Illustrated by the author

Sonlight Curriculum Ltd.

Requests for permission to make copies of any part of the work should be
mailed to: Permissions Department, Harcourt Brace Jovanovich, Publishers,
Orlando, Florida 32887.

Library of Congress Cataloging-in-Publication Data
Lattimore, Eleanor Frances.
Little Pear : the story of a little Chinese boy/written and
illustrated by Eleanor Frances Lattimore.
p.   cm.

Summary: The adventures of Little Pear, a mischievous
five-year-old boy living in China in the early 1900s.
ISBN 1-887840-15-X

Printed in the United States of America

This Sonlight Curriculum, Ltd. edition first published 1996.
3 5 7 9 8 6 4 2
99 01 03 05 07 08 06 04 02 00

For a catalog of Sonlight Curriculum materials for the home school, contact
Sonlight Curriculum, Ltd.
8042 South Grant Way
Littleton, CO 80122-2705
USA

http://www.sonlight-curriculum.com

CONTENTS

1

Little Pear and His Family

There was once a Chinese boy called Little Pear.
He lived with his father, his mother, and his
two sisters in a small house at the edge of a village
in China. All around the village were flat fields of
cabbages and beans and onions, and far away on
one side was a great highway that led to the city,
and far away on the other side was a river. Little
Pear's mother used to say to him, "You may run
and play out-of-doors, but do not go too near the
river. You might fall in." Sometimes, though, Little

Pear would disobey his mother. He loved to stand on the high bank and look down on the swift muddy river and the ships sailing down it toward the sea. He would hold very tight to a huge willow tree with both hands and think, "I can never fall in—not if I am very careful, like this."

Little Pear was a very mischievous child. His sisters said he was naughty. His father said he was naughty and would cry, "Ay-ah! What a bad boy you are!" But his mother said, "He is very little; when he gets bigger he will be good; you wait and see. It doesn't matter if he is naughty now, sometimes!" And they all loved Little Pear very much.

Little Pear was five years old. He had a round, solemn face with eyes like black apple seeds. He didn't look mischievous at all. His head was shaved, except for one round spot just over his forehead where the hair was allowed to grow and was braided into a little pigtail tied with bright-colored string. His mother thought this looked very beautiful. He was always very gaily dressed in flowered jackets buttoned down the front, and striped trousers tied in around the ankles with wide strips of cloth.

The two sisters of Little Pear were very good little girls. One was called Dagu, because she was the biggest; and the other was called Ergu, because she was the second one. They both wore jackets and

The house

trousers like Little Pear, but you could tell that they
were girls instead of boys because they wore tiny
gold earrings and because their jackets buttoned
down the side. Dagu's hair was braided into one
long braid, and Ergu's was parted in the middle and
braided into two shorter ones. Dagu was quiet and
gentle and helped her mother about the house, and
when Little Pear was a baby it was Dagu who carried
him around on her back and taught him nursery
rhymes. But when Little Pear grew older it was Ergu
who played with him the most, for she was only two
years older than he, and she was a tomboy besides.

The house that Little Pear lived in, like the other houses in the village, was made of sun-baked bricks the color of dust. There was only one room, with an earthen floor and paper windows. You couldn't see through the windows unless you poked your finger through the paper, but they made the room a little lighter. There was one door, with a little window in it, that led into the courtyard in front of the house. All around the courtyard there was a high wall, and in it there was a gateway leading to the street. There were two stone lions in front of the gateway, on either side of the red-painted door. They had curly manes,

and mouths that looked as though they might be laughing or might be roaring; Little Pear could never decide which.

The house was at the end of the street and at the edge of the village. You could stand in the gateway and look across the flat fields toward the river. You could not see the river, but you could

see the tall masts and sails of the ships. It gave Little Pear a happy feeling to stand there and think of the river and of the sea and of the whole world! His little pigtail would stand straight up with excitement!

Inside the house there was very little furniture. The family all slept on a huge square bed made of gray bricks and built against the wall. It was wide and flat and hard. The pillows were shaped like long rolls, and they were hard too; but Little Pear and his family rolled themselves up in their warm quilts and slept very comfortably. There was a brick stove at the back of the room where Little Pear's mother cooked the meals, and there was also a fireplace under the bed. In the winter they had a fire burning

there to keep them warm. During the day they put a small table with short legs on top of the bed and gathered there for meals.

Their only pet was a yellow bird, who sang sweetly from his cage which swung by the open doorway.

2

Little Pear Sees the City

One winter day when the sun was shining brightly and the frost lay on the hard ground, Little Pear said, "Oh, Mother! I am going out to play. I will take very good care of myself."

His mother put two extra coats on him, with quilted linings, and a cap with flaps over the ears. "Run along and have a good time. Don't fall!" And she laughed as he disappeared through the front gate, because he looked so funny and fat in all his padded coats. Even if he should fall down, he couldn't possibly feel the bump.

Little Pear ran down the village street. "Come and play!" he called to his friends.

His friends were all out playing along the street. Some were playing tag, and some were tossing shuttlecocks, while others were watching from their doorways. "You play with us," they called to Little Pear.

"Oh, no!" he answered. "I am going to the pond on the other side of the village. I am going to slide!" And he ran on.

Soon he came to the house of his friend Big Head. He looked inside the courtyard. There was Big Head, with his baby brother on his back. "Big Head!" he called, "will you play with me? I am going to slide on the pond!"

Big Head was Little Pear's best friend. He was a little older than Little Pear. He had a round solemn face too, and his head was shaved, like Little Pear's.

But instead of only one pigtail, Big Head had three—one over his forehead and one over each ear. He shook his head sadly when Little Pear asked him to come and slide. "I cannot come," he replied. "My mother has gone to market and I am minding my baby brother. Will you stay with me?"

"Not now," said Little Pear, "for the sun is shining and I must go and slide." And he ran on.

At the end of the village Little Pear almost bumped into a friendly pig. "Pig," he said, "you should look where you are going! Do you want to come and slide with me?"

But the pig didn't understand, so Little Pear ran on, down a path and across a field, until he came to the pond.

"This is fun!" he thought, and he began to slide. He slid and slid, and the wind came up and blew him about like a tiny ship. Sometimes he fell down—kerflop!—but he was so bundled up that he couldn't feel the bumps. 'I should like to be a boat and sail down the river," thought Little Pear, "or I should like to be a kite and fly up in the sky—but, ay-ah! It is fun to be a little boy and slide on the pond!"

Just then there was a great noise, as several boys appeared from the village and ran toward the

pond, followed by a puppy. They fastened on some skates, which were flat pieces of wood. Each boy had only one skate, which he slid along on, pushing himself with the other foot. They started across the pond toward Little Pear, shouting, while the puppy scampered and slid at their heels, barking loudly. The biggest boy had a long pole with a spike on the end of it. He pushed it between his legs, and this made him go very fast. Before Little Pear could blink his eyes the big boy had come up to him. "What are you doing on our pond?" he cried. "This is no place for little fellows like you. Go away home to your mother!" This made Little Pear so angry that he sat down hard, but he said as proudly as he could, "I can skate, too!" The other boys came sliding up and circled around him, and the puppy looked inquiringly in his face. They laughed when Little Pear said that he could skate. "You cannot skate when you are sitting down," they said rudely, "and besides, you have no skates!"

Little Pear wanted to cry, but instead he picked himself up and trotted to the edge of the pond. Then he turned around, and "When I grow up I will spank you!" he cried.

The big boys continued to skate in circles around the pond, and Little Pear started sadly for home. Suddenly he stopped. No, it would never do to go

home now, when it was such a fine day. He didn't want to go home; there was too much to see out-of-doors. He turned back across the field in the direction of the highroad.

The highroad was really high. If you stood on one side of it you couldn't see what lay on the other side. But after you had climbed up the path to the top of the highroad you could look down at the flat fields on the other side, and see away in the distance the small dust-colored houses of other villages.

The highroad stretched across the fields for miles and miles. It led into villages and out of villages, and still it kept going. Little Pear knew that if he followed it he would reach the city; and he wished that his legs were not so short. On either side of the highroad there were trees. There was a row of peach trees first and then a row of willow trees behind them. In the spring they were very beautiful, but now it was winter, and the wind swept along the highroad and crackled their branches.

Little Pear began to feel hungry, but there were so many sights to see as he trudged along that he didn't remember how long it was since he had eaten. Rickshaws went by, with richly dressed people riding in them. Little Pear wondered how the men who pulled the rickshaws could run so fast, because some of them had very heavy loads. In one there was a fat man with several bundles, and in another there was a whole family riding, a mother with three children. Yet the men who pulled them ran so quickly that they all soon left Little Pear far behind.

Carts went by, and men traveling with bundles slung over their shoulders. Little Pear looked longingly at the carts and wished that he might ride in one. They were fine carts, with two great wooden wheels, and sides and rounded top covered with blue cloth. The drivers sat in the open front with their legs crossed lazily and sometimes flicked the horses with long whips they held, with red tassels on the end. The carts plodded along slowly, but even they went more quickly than Little Pear.

Little Pear trudged along and wondered how far away the city was. Suddenly a man passed him and stopped. "Where are you going, little traveler? You are very small to be alone on this great highroad," he said. The man was tall and young and had a kind face. He wore a long blue gown, with a black satin

waistcoat over it. On his head he had a small round
black hat, with a braided button on top.

Little Pear looked at him and smiled. "I am
going with you," he said.

"But I am going to the city. It is too far for short
legs like yours."

Then Little Pear looked very sad. "I have never
seen the city," he said. "Can I get there and back
by sunset?"

The kind man asked him where his home was,
and when Little Pear told him that it was in the
village of Shegu he was very much astonished. "But
that is a long way! How far you have walked! We
are nearer to the city." And he lifted Little Pear to

He could see the whole world, nearly

his shoulders, saying, "I will take you with me, and when we reach the city I will send you home by a friend of mine who has a cart."

Little Pear was very happy. From the shoulders of the tall man he could see the whole world, nearly. This was a great adventure, and he kept thinking, "How proud Ergu will be to know that her brother is a traveler!"

Jingle, jingle, jingle! A donkey trotted by with bells around his neck and gay saddlebags. A man was sitting on his back, and he smiled at Little Pear. "Should you like a ride?" he asked.

"I am riding!" replied Little Pear, and he held tight to his new friend and laughed as the donkey tinkled away into the distance.

The sun was setting, but Little Pear had forgotten that he should be at home. He was growing sleepy and hungry, but he kept thinking, "I am seeing the world!"

At last the tall man said, "Look! There is the great city!" Little Pear sat up straight with a jerk, and looked. There, not very far away, were the high gray walls of the city. The highroad led straight up to the city gate. It was a huge archway, and above it was a tower with a roof of curved tiles. As Little Pear and his friend drew nearer, the city walls seemed to grow higher; and as they were about to enter the gate, the tower above it seemed to reach the sky.

Inside the city walls there were crowds of people filling the streets. There was a tremendous bustle of carts, rickshaws, and traveling men selling their wares. Everyone was in the middle of the street, as there were no sidewalks. The shops along the street had open fronts, so that you could see what was inside them. There were food shops and basket shops and lantern shops and silk shops, and every other kind of shop you could possibly imagine. Lights blazed out from inside the shops, and red and gold signs and banners swung in front of them. There was so much noise and so many lights that it made Little Pear blink. He meant to say, "I like the city!" but instead he said, "I am so hungry!"

It was a huge archway

The kind man took him to a shop where there were round trays heaped high with steamed dumplings, fresh and hot, and other trays filled with delicious twisted breads. When Little Pear had eaten all that he could hold he fell fast asleep.

Late that night a cart rattled into the village of Shegu; and the driver stopped at the first house to ask if a little boy had been lost. The family ran out in great excitement. "Little Pear, the son of Mr. Huang, ran away today!" they cried. "Perhaps it is he!" and they peeked inside the cart. There, wrapped in a warm quilt, was Little Pear, sleeping soundly.

They showed the driver of the cart the house

Banners swung in front of them

where Little Pear's family lived, and Little Pear was soon safe in the arms of his mother, with all his family about him, and as many of the neighbors as the small house would hold. "You were a naughty boy to run away," said his father; and his mother said, "Ay-ah! He was very naughty, but I am so glad to have him back that we shall not spank him this time." And they all crowded around Little Pear and asked him many questions.

"Oh, Little Pear," cried Ergu excitedly, "what did you see in the city?"

"I ate some dumplings," replied Little Pear sleepily.

3

How Little Pear Wanted Both
a Top and a Tang-hulur

For some time after Little Pear's trip to the city he was very good. Perhaps he was sorry to have frightened his family so. Anyway, he was very good, and one day his mother said, "Little Pear, here are some pennies. Run along and buy yourself a pretty toy."

"Thank you!" said Little Pear, reaching out in delight for the pennies. They had holes in the middle and were all strung on a string which was tied so that they could not slip off. Little Pear started forth in great excitement, almost tripping over the high doorstep. As he hurried along the street he counted his pennies—one, two, three, four—four pennies! He couldn't remember ever having been so rich before.

On each side of the street were walls made of sun-baked bricks. Over the top of the walls you could see the roofs of the houses. Some were made of gray tiles, and some were made of straw. In the walls were many gateways, leading into the courtyards of the houses. They had different colored doors: red doors and black doors and once in a while a green door dotted with gold paint.

"Little Pear! Little Pear!" called a voice suddenly. Little Pear turned around, and there was his friend Big Head, calling to him from his gateway. "Come and see my new top!" he cried. "It is the most beautiful top in the whole world, and the fastest spinner!"

"Ay-ah!" exclaimed Little Pear, and he looked at the top admiringly. It was certainly a beauty—a

great pear-shaped silver top, with stripes of scarlet, pink, and green.

Big Head proudly spun it, and it twirled round and round, while a crowd of children gathered to watch. Little Pear slipped away toward the street where the shops were, thinking, "Perhaps I can find a beautiful top like that! I have four pennies."

Little Pear walked along the street, humming happily, and the very first shop that he came to sold tinware. There were little tin teapots and tin sauce-pans, and they hung in bunches in front of the open shop and rattled merrily in the breeze. Little Pear

stopped and looked at the tinware and thought that he would like a teapot of his own. But then he looked at his four pennies and thought of the top, and so he walked on.

"Hot chestnuts, hot chestnuts!"

"Hot chestnuts, hot chestnuts!" called a man in a loud sing-sing voice, standing behind a tray of smoking hot chestnuts, just off the charcoal. Little Pear wrinkled his nose in joy as he sniffed the delicious smell. But he looked at his four pennies and thought of the toy shop at the end of the street, and he walked on.

"Tang-hulurs! Tang-hulurs!" called a man coming toward him, and this time Little Pear stopped short with his mouth wide open.

For the man was simply laden down with tang-hulurs, which were Little Pear's favorite candy. He looked at the red fruit, eight or ten on a stick, all covered with candied syrup, and he jingled his string of pennies. He thought that he would be perfectly happy if he could have a tang-hulur.

"How much?" he asked the man.

"Two pennies a stick!"

Little Pear untied the string and gave the man

The toy shop

two of his precious pennies. Then he started on toward the toy shop, nibbling at his tang-hulur.

The toy shop was very wonderful. There were wooden swords painted in pink and green and gold. There were funny little monkeys made of clay covered over with chicken feathers, and round boxes made of gourds, all delicately carved. The boxes were stained orange or green or brown, and they had crickets inside of them that made a queer little singing noise with their wings. There were cloth

tigers, with smiling faces and green glass eyes. And, yes, there were tops! Tops of all colors, striped and plain.

"This one," said Little Pear to the shopman, pointing to one as large and beautiful as Big Head's.

"The tops," said the man, "are four pennies."

"Oh, dear! Oh, dear!" cried Little Pear, "and I bought a tang-hulur with two of my pennies! There are not enough left."

"Come back someday when you have more money," said the shopman; but suddenly Little Pear had a much better idea. He ran down the street until he met the tang-hulur man again.

"Another tang-hulur, please!" he said, and handed the man his last two pennies in exchange for another delicious stick of candy.

Then very happily he trotted along till he came to the home of Big Head. Big Head was sitting on his doorstep alone, holding his top. He looked very much surprised when he saw Little Pear with two tang-hulurs.

One tang-hulur was almost gone, but the other hadn't had a single bite taken out of it. "Oh, Little Pear, how good they must taste!" said Big Head. "I do love tang-hulurs!"

"So do I," replied Little Pear, "but I will trade

you my whole tang-hulur that isn't eaten for your
top."

But that Big Head would not do. He was a little
older and wiser than Little Pear; so he said, "I

cannot give you my precious top, but I will share it with you if you will share your tang-hulur with me."

So that is what they did. They took turns eating the tang-hulur until it was gone, and then they took turns spinning the top, and they were perfectly happy.

4

How Little Pear Lit a Firecracker

Crack—crack—crack! Firecrackers were popping, gongs were ringing, and all through the village there were crowds of people coming and going. For the New Year's festival had started. In China they celebrate the New Year for two whole weeks, and all during that time everybody has a holiday.

"This is the time of good things to eat," said Little Pear to Ergu, as they sat on the high doorstep of their gateway, between the two stone lions. They were happily munching some round flat cakes, and listening to the jolly noise of firecrackers coming from farther down the street.

"I wish the New Year's festival would last forever!" said Ergu. "Nobody has to work now, and tonight there are going to be very beautiful fireworks—and we all have new clothes!"

Little Pear looked proudly down at his new mustard-colored trousers and purple jacket. He had a bright green string tied around his pigtail, and he wore a silver chain around his neck with a dragon clasp in front. It was a good-luck chain. His mother hoped that it would keep him from running away.

Ergu, too, had on new clothes. She had on a bright red jacket and bright red trousers, and down her forehead there were three spots of red paint, which were just meant for trimming, and made her look very pretty.

Crack—crack—crack! The firecrackers were popping steadily farther down the street. Suddenly Little Pear jumped up. "I am going to watch them!" he cried. "You may finish my cake."

"Don't go too near the firecrackers!" called Ergu as Little Pear ran off. "Take care, because you have on your new clothes!"

Little Pear ran along, and the farther he got from home and the nearer to the middle of the village, the more people there were. The streets were crowded with people, all smiling and happy, for everyone was having a holiday. Little Pear pushed his way through the crowd, taking care not to step on any chickens or to tumble over any babies. In the very center of the village was the biggest crowd of all; for there in the middle of the street was a man who was setting off firecrackers—small ones and big ones and middle-sized ones. Firecrackers that were separate and went off—pop! and firecrackers that were all strung together and went pop-pop-pop-pop-pop!

All the boys of the village were standing around the man, watching him with their mouths open.

"Stand back!" he said to them. "Don't come too close. It is dangerous to come too near to the firecrackers. Stand around in a circle, and not so close."

Little Pear pushed his way through the crowd quite easily, he was so small. Soon he was standing at the edge of the circle, where he could see all the firecrackers very plainly as they went off. He stood and watched excitedly as the man lit the firecrackers one by one from a piece of punk. "How I should like to light one!" he thought.

Just then a big boy spoke to the man. "Let me set off a firecracker!" he begged. "I want to set off

Little Pear pushed his way through the crowd

a big one with a very loud bang." Little Pear looked
up at the boy. It was the biggest of the boys who
had chased him off the pond.

When the man said to the boy, "Yes, you may
light just one firecracker," Little Pear thought, "Perhaps he will let me light just one too if I ask him.
That will show that I am a big boy, too."

The big boy struck a match and lighted a large
firecracker. Then he stepped back quickly. "Bang!"

went the cracker, shooting up into the air. "Ay-ah!" cried everybody. "What a beautiful firecracker that one was! And what a loud noise it made!"

"Please," said Little Pear to the man, "may I light a firecracker, too?"

"You are too small," said the man.

"You are too small," said the big boy; and everybody else said, "Oh, yes, he is too small."

Then Little Pear said, "Why, no! I am not too small. I can light a small firecracker!"

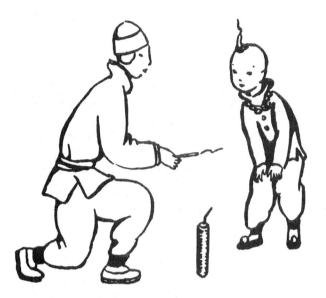

The man laughed in a kind way. "All right," he said, "you may light one. But be very quick and very careful."

Little Pear picked out a tiny firecracker. Then he stood it up in the middle of the circle and drew in his breath as he leaned over and lighted it. "Stand back, everyone!" he cried. But in his excitement Little Pear forgot to stand back himself. "Pop!" went the firecracker, and it flew right up and hit Little Pear!

"Oh!" cried Little Pear—and "Oh!" cried everybody else. "Are you hurt? Did it burn you?"

"No," said Little Pear in rather a surprised voice,

"Stand back, everyone!"

but he looked down at his clothes, and there, right in the middle of his very best, brand-new purple jacket was a hole burnt by the firecracker!

"Oh!" cried Little Pear, more loudly this time. "My beautiful new jacket!" He suddenly remem-

bered that Ergu had told him not to go too near the firecrackers, and he felt so ashamed that he began to cry. The people all tried to comfort him.

"Never mind," they said. "That was a fine firecracker that you set off! And as for the hole, why, your mother will mend it so that it will not even show."

Little Pear felt better then, and he thought that if he was a big enough boy to fire off a firecracker, he was too big a boy to cry. He pushed his way through the crowd again, in the direction of his house. He was taking care again not to bump into any babies or to step on any chickens—when all of a sudden, bump! Somebody ran into him. It was Ergu.

"Oh, Little Pear!" she cried, "I have been looking for you. Father has brought us some beautiful new kites for New Year's presents. Come quickly and see."

When Ergu and Little Pear reached home, there, sure enough, were the kites. One was like a huge yellow butterfly, and one was like a giant goldfish. Little Pear was so delighted that he forgot all about his new jacket until his mother said, "I smell something burnt." Then he remembered.

"It's my new jacket," he said, his voice growing very small. "I lit a firecracker, just one; but it burnt a hole in my new jacket."

"Oh, Little Pear, what a bad boy you are!" cried his mother. "But I am glad that it is only your jacket that is hurt, and not you. Firecrackers are very dangerous, and you must never, never, light one again! At least, not until you are a very big boy."

That night the family stood in their doorway, watching the fireworks that were to celebrate the New Year's festival. All the sky over the village was bright with the beautiful many-colored lights. Little Pear and his sisters were all dressed in their very best new clothes, but if you looked closely at Little Pear's purple jacket you could see a tiny hole, neatly darned. As he heard the hissing noise of the skyrockets and watched the sparks falling across the sky, Little Pear decided that when he was a very big boy he would send off one million firecrackers and two million skyrockets—but that now, after all, it was nearly as much fun to watch!

How Ergu Lost Her Kite and Almost Lost Little Pear

One day during the New Year's festival Ergu said to Little Pear, "Let us take our new kites out to the field and fly them. It is such a windy day that they will fly very high." Little Pear hopped with joy, because he had never had such a beautiful big kite before. He could hardly wait to see it flying up in the sky.

"Be careful, children," called their mother from the gateway as they started off toward the field.

"Ergu, take care of Little Pear! And, Little Pear, don't lose your kite!"

She watched the children as they left the village and started out across the field, and smiled, because Chinese mothers like to have their children fly kites. They believe that good spirits fly down to them along the kite-strings and that evil spirits fly away from them up into the sky.

The children chattered happily as they walked along. When they reached the middle of the field they stopped. "This will be a good place," said Ergu. "There are no trees anywhere near that can tangle our kites, and feel how the wind blows here! They will go very high."

Ergu's kite, the huge yellow butterfly, was nearly as big as she—but Little Pear's kite, the giant gold-fish, was so huge that when he carried it you couldn't see any little boy at all. As they unwound the string the wind pulled the kites with great jerks as though it wanted to pull them away. Ergu and Little Pear held tight to the sticks and unwound the string carefully, never letting go for one second.

Soon the yellow butterfly was way up in the sky. "Oh, oh!" cried Ergu. "How beautiful it is! Little Pear, you are very slow. Hurry, and let your kite go up as high as mine. Then they can talk to each other."

Little Pear couldn't reply, because it took all his breath to hold on to his kite-string. The wind tugged and pulled it so hard that it almost made him lose his balance. He sat down on the ground and held on tight and wondered if he'd soon be flying, too! And he patiently unwound the rest of his string.

Ergu was running about the field, looking over her shoulder at her kite that was sailing swiftly across the sky. "Oh, Little Pear!" she cried. "This is such fun! This is just like flying myself!" And then she

stopped suddenly, and her eyes and mouth all grew very round, for what did she see? There was poor Little Pear holding tightly to his kite-string, and the wind was tugging at his huge kite, and carrying it farther and farther up into the sky—and Little Pear along with it! His toes were off the ground, but he still held tight to his kite-string. "Oh, Little Pear!" cried Ergu, and before she knew it she had let go of her own beautiful yellow butterfly and rushed to

the rescue of her small brother. The wind was carrying him along so quickly that she thought she
could never catch up with him! The wind blew the
kite, and blew Little Pear, but it blew Ergu, too.

With the wind behind her she ran very fast. At
last she caught hold of Little Pear's jacket—then
she caught hold of Little Pear himself! And then
they both sat down on the ground. "I wonder if we
shall both be blown away now," thought Ergu; but
no, the two of them were too strong for the wind.
They stayed right where they were. Then together
Ergu and Little Pear wound the string around the

They both sat down on the ground

stick again, and carefully, carefully, drew the kite down from the sky.

When the huge goldfish lay on the ground at last and Little Pear was winding up the last part of the string, Ergu looked up at the sky

where her butterfly was a yellow speck and felt very sad indeed. "But I'm glad it wasn't Little Pear that disappeared," she thought, "and he very nearly did!"

"Were you good children?" asked their mother when they returned home. "Oh, yes, we were very good!" cried Ergu and Little Pear together. "I didn't lose my kite!" said Little Pear. "I took care of Little Pear!" said Ergu.

And they were so hungry from playing

in the wind that they ate a very large supper
of fried cornmeal, bean sprouts, and hot tea.

6

How Little Pear Ate Some
Green Peaches

It was a warm spring day. The peach trees along
the highroad had bloomed, and now the trees were
laden with small green peaches. The willows were
pale green with their feathery new leaves.

In the fields the farmers were working. Water
was running swiftly through the ditches they had
cut, criss-crossing the fields. These ditches were
meant to water the onions, the beans, the cabbages,
and all the other vegetables, but the children of the

village thought that they made splendid rivers for toy ships.

Little Pear and his friend Big Head each had a ship. They were made out of kaoliang, which is a kind of millet. The outside of the stalks can be peeled off in strips, and with these strips, and the pith inside, Chinese children make all sorts of toys. Little Pear and Big Head were racing the ships that they had made, but they were sometimes interrupted by the farmers. "Go away!" they would shout. "Bad boys! You are trampling on our vegetables!" And then Big Head and Little Pear would move away very quickly to a part of the field that was farther off and start another race.

"Big Head," said Little Pear, "let's pretend that

this ditch is the Yellow River. My ship is a junk
with three sails and I will race you to the next turn."

"My ship has seven sails," cried Big Head, and
he put his piece of kaoliang in the ditch right beside
Little Pear's, and the boats started off down the great
Yellow River. The water carried the little boats along
rapidly, and the two boys ran along the banks, calling out excitedly, "Mine's ahead!" "No, mine!" "Mine
is now!" "There goes mine!" And they didn't notice

that they were drawing nearer and nearer to a very angry farmer.

Suddenly: "Chuba!" shouted the farmer. "Go away! How dare you trample on my vegetables? Run quick, or I will beat you!"

Big Head and Little Pear were so astonished that they forgot all about their race. They forgot that their boats were sailing the Yellow River. They started to run very fast.

"Chuba!" cried the farmer again, and he began to chase them. He was a tall man with a shaved head, and he had long legs. Big Head and Little Pear didn't look at him closely, but they thought that he looked rather fierce. They ran and ran. They ran in the direction of the highroad. Little Pear looked over his shoulder once, but then he went on running faster than ever, because the farmer was

carrying a hoe. This made him look more fierce than before. "If—we—reach—the—highroad," said Big Head between puffs, "we—can—hide on the other side." Little Pear nodded, but he couldn't say anything because he was rather fat and he had never run so fast before.

By and by they reached the highroad and looked behind them. The farmer had stopped chasing them and had gone back to his work.

"He—was—only—trying—to—frighten—us," said Big Head, still puffing. Little Pear nodded.

They sat down to rest under the nearest tree, and pretty soon they remembered their race.

"I wonder where our junks are now," said Little Pear. "Perhaps the race is over," said Big Head. "I think mine won."

"No, I'm sure mine did!"

But they didn't feel like going back just then to see.

"Look," said Little Pear suddenly. "Do you see anything in the tree above us?"

"Yes," said Big Head, "peaches!"

And sure enough, the tree was laden with peaches, but they were green.

"I wonder if they taste good," said Little Pear. "I should like to eat some, for I am very, very hungry."

Big Head was a little older than Little Pear, and a little wiser. "They would give you a very bad tummyache," he said.

Little Pear sighed. He thought that just one peach couldn't possibly hurt, and he felt hungrier all the time. "Big Head," he said, "I shall eat just one peach, and then if it doesn't hurt me, I can eat some more." Big Head agreed that one peach would probably not hurt anyone; so they found a stick and poked the tree. No peaches fell.

"They are stuck too tight," said Big Head. "Wait a minute! I will climb the tree!" Big Head started climbing, but every time he climbed a little way he slid back a little way. "This is a very hard tree to climb," said Big Head.

"I know," said Little Pear. "Put your hands on your knees and I will climb on your back."

"That is a good idea," said Big Head. So he put his hands on his knees, and Little Pear climbed on his back; and just as Little Pear had gathered three peaches, Big Head fell down with Little Pear on top of him!

When they were right side up again they col-
lected the peaches. Big Head said that he didn't
want any, not even one, and that Little Pear could
have them all. "But be careful," he said. "If the
first one hurts you, do not eat the others." So Little
Pear ate the first one carefully, while Big Head
watched him anxiously. "Does it taste good?" he
asked.

"Yes," replied Little Pear, "and it doesn't make
me feel bad at all. I don't think another one would
hurt me." So he ate the second. Then he looked at
the last one for a while, and it was so small that he

Big Head fell down with Little Pear on top of him!

finally ate that, too. He and Big Head decided that
perhaps green peaches were good for children.

But later in the day Little Pear's mother said to
him, "You do not look very well"; and when he
wouldn't eat his supper, which was steamed dumplings stuffed with cabbage, with bean sauce, she
said, "This child must be ill." Then she put him to
bed. All night long Little Pear tossed and turned in
his far corner of the wide, hard bed. In his sleep
he kept talking about fierce farmers, and peaches,
and the Yellow River: and junks, and a hoe, and
peaches—and he was very ill.

Next morning Big Head came to see him, looking rather worried. "What happened?" he asked.

Little Pear shook his head sadly. "Green peaches are not good for children, after all," he said.

When Little Pear was well again he and Big Head sailed their boats many more times in the ditches and had many more races, but neither of them *ever* ate green peaches again.

7

How the Canary Flew Away

"Cheep, cheep, cheep!" sang the canary in his cage near the doorway. "Cheep, cheep!" And he jumped from his perch to his swing and back again.

Little Pear looked up at the bird from his seat on the doorstep. "I wish I knew what it is you are saying!" he said.

"Cheep, cheep!" replied the bird, cocking his head on one side and looking down inquiringly at Little Pear.

"He is talking to me," thought Little Pear, and he got up quickly and tugged a stool over to the cage and climbed up on it so that he could see the bird better. "What are you saying?" he asked. "Are you hungry? Why, there is your dish all filled with seeds and you haven't eaten them!"

"Cheep, cheep," said the bird.

"Perhaps he is thirsty," thought Little Pear, and he looked in the other dish; but no, there was plenty of water there. "There can be nothing the matter with you, foolish little bird," said Little Pear severely. "You have food and you have water and you have a beautiful cage."

But the canary said "cheep," this time so sadly that Little Pear knew that he wanted something.

The sun was shining brightly, and it was nearly summer. The fields around the village were green with growing vegetables. Little Pear climbed down off the stool and stood in the doorway. He looked across the sunny courtyard and through the open gateway to the world outside. From where he stood he could see the green fields and far away beyond them the row of green willow trees by the river. The world seemed very wide and very beautiful. High up in the sky were some small white clouds sailing lazily along. Some pigeons flew by,

"Cheep, cheep," said the bird

and as Little Pear watched them he heard music. They were tame pigeons, whose owners let them fly about; but first they had tied queer little reed whistles to their tails. As the pigeons flew through the air the wind played music on their whistles. "What a good time the pigeons are having!" thought Little Pear. He watched them until they had flown out of sight behind a curved roof, and then he turned back to look at the little bird in its cage. "I know what you want to do," he said. "You want to fly away!"

"Cheep, cheep, cheep!" said the canary excit-

"You want to fly away!"

edly, and Little Pear climbed on the
stool again and pushed up the door
of the cage.

"Come back by and by!" he said.
But the canary was in so much of a
hurry to fly away, across the fields
and into the sky, that it didn't even wait to say
"cheep."

Later that day the family was gathering
for the afternoon meal. "I must feed the
bird, too," said Dagu.
But when she   looked
up at the cage she saw
that it was empty. "Oh,
where has our canary
gone?" she cried.

"He flew away,"
said Little Pear.

"You naughty boy, did you open the door of the
cage?"

"Yes," said Little Pear anxiously, "because he
asked to go."

"Will he ever come back to us?" asked Ergu.

"I told him to," said Little Pear.

The family were all sorrowful because their
little bird was gone. Each day the children looked at

the empty cage and watched the sky to see whether the bird was flying back. When one day their father came home with a brand-new cage with a little yellow bird inside it, the children jumped up and down with delight.

"Cheep, cheep, cheep!" the little bird was singing.

"He *did* come back," cried Little Pear.

"It's the very same bird," cried Ergu.

And perhaps it was.

8

How Little Pear Went to the Fair

The men in the village of Shegu, where Little Pear and his family lived, were mostly farmers. All day they worked in the fields that lay on all sides of the village. Sometimes they would go to market fairs at neighboring villages to sell their grain and vegetables and to buy what they needed from other farmers.

Little Pear's father was a farmer. One day in the summer he came in from the fields very early. "There is a fair today," he said, "in the village of Wuku. I am going there to sell some of my onions and cabbages and to buy some melons and sweet potatoes. I have heard that it is a very large fair, with many things to buy besides vegetables. So I shall bring a present to each of the children when I come home."

Dagu, Ergu, and Little Pear all became very much excited. Dagu loved pretty things to wear. "I should like some silk flowers to put in my hair," she said.

Ergu liked bright-colored things to play with. "I should like a lantern," she said, "shaped like a fish or like a rabbit."

Little Pear said nothing, because what he wanted most of all was to go to the fair himself. While the others were talking he slipped out into the courtyard.

The village of Wuku was three miles away. Little Pear's father was going to walk there, pushing his wheelbarrow full of vegetables. The wheelbarrow stood in the courtyard, all ready and laden with the

onions and cabbages. Little Pear walked around the wheelbarrow, looking to see whether there was any space anywhere big enough for a small boy to squeeze into. And, yes! There was one. Little Pear crawled in among four cabbages and covered himself up as well as he could with some onions. Then he lay very still.

When Little Pear's father started out in the direction of Wuku it seemed to him that his wheelbarrow was rather heavy, but he only thought, "What a fine load of vegetables I have!" He never guessed that Little Pear was hidden in the load.

"Where is Little Pear?" asked Ergu, after she and Dagu had watched their father out of sight.

"That naughty boy!" said Dagu. "He is always up to some mischief."

"I hope he hasn't run away," said his mother anxiously. But then she remembered that Little Pear had on his silver good-luck chain. "He has probably just gone to play with Big Head," she said, and went back to her work in the house.

Dagu and Ergu went back to their work, too. They sat on the doorstep, sewing, while the canary sang and hopped around in his cage above them. They were making shoes—shoes of black cloth, with soles made of layers and layers of white cloth, stitched together very firmly. As they embroidered flowers

and butterflies on the toes of their black shoes and stitched the cloth soles, they thought of the fair and hoped that their father would return soon.

Meanwhile, their father was jogging along a rough country road with his wheelbarrow, and Little Pear was curled up tight among the cabbages and onions. He was lying very still, for he was afraid that if his father should discover him he would send him home. Little Pear thought, "I shouldn't mind being spanked—so very much; but I *do* want to see the fair!"

Joggetty, joggetty, jog. The wheelbarrow went bumping along the rough road. Little Pear wanted to poke his head out, to see the countryside as they passed. But he thought that he had better keep still. From where he lay he could hear all sorts of strange sounds on all sides of him. There were donkey bells, and the jingling of traveling tinkers. There was the creaking of cart wheels, the grunting of pigs, and every once in a while there was the braying of a donkey. There were many footsteps, and voices—loud and high, and old and young. "There are lots of people going to the fair," thought Little Pear.

Joggetty, joggetty, jog. Then suddenly the wheelbarrow stopped. "Is this the fair?" Little Pear wondered, and he peeped out very cautiously from under the onions with one black apple-seed eye. Yes, they had reached the village of Wuku. It looked just like Little Pear's own village, only it was more crowded than his had been even during the New Year's festival. On every side were the people who had come to buy and sell. There were young men with round smiling faces. There were old men with high wrinkled foreheads and thin gray beards. There were farmers and merchant-men and fruit-growers, and men who sold pigs or sheep, and men who sold birds.

The fair was all along the main street of the village. Fruit and vegetables were arranged in tempting piles along both sides of the street. There were trays of candy, too—the thin flat kind made of sesame seeds stuck together with syrup, and cut in squares; the square black kind that looked like charcoal; and best of all, tang-hulurs.

There were men selling all sorts of things besides food. There were men with bundles that they untied and spread out along the sides of the street. Some of these bundles were filled with porcelain dishes, and some were filled with beads. Some had small square chests in them, with little drawers filled with

curious things—small people carved out of wood, and tiny silver fishes that wriggled as though they were alive.

Little Pear saw everything as well as he could from his hiding place. He was peeping out with both eyes now, but nobody noticed him because everybody was too busy buying and selling. The middle of the street was thronged with people, all jostling each other, and each man calling out in a loud voice the name of the thing he was selling.

"Perhaps I can climb out of this wheelbarrow without being seen," thought Little Pear, but just then there was a sudden disturbance. A man who had brought some pigs to sell was trying to pass a man with a flock of sheep. The sheep and the pigs

were all getting mixed up, and the two men were angry and excited. Each one shouted out that it was the other's fault. The sheep bleated, the pigs grunted, and Little Pear, who was watching, suddenly began to laugh.

"What is the matter with your onions?" asked a farmer, who had stopped to buy from Little Pear's father. "Your onions have a voice; they are laughing."

Little Pear's father grew very angry. "Some bad boy has hidden himself under my wheelbarrow," he said. And he looked under the wheelbarrow. There was no one there.

"Look inside," suggested the farmer. So Little Pear's father lifted up the onions—and there was Little Pear!

By this time a crowd of people had gathered around the wheelbarrow. They all laughed loudly when they saw what was inside. "Did he grow on your farm?" they asked Little Pear's father. "You

They all stared at Little Pear

must have a very remarkable farm!" Then they all laughed again, and they all stared at Little Pear, who sat among the cabbages with his pigtail standing straight up in the air.

Little Pear's father started to be angry, but when he saw that everybody thought it was a joke he laughed, too. "This is not for sale," he said, patting Little Pear on the head, "but the rest is."

The men were all in a good humor now. They started to buy the cabbages and onions. Soon everything was sold, and Little Pear's father had an empty wheelbarrow and several strings of money. "Perhaps it is a good thing that you came," he said to Little Pear. "Now I shall buy some sweet potatoes and some melons."

When they returned home that evening Little Pear rode in the wheelbarrow again, but this time he sat on top of the load instead of being hidden. In one hand he held a present for Dagu—some beautiful silk flowers fastened on long pins to put in her hair. In his other hand was the present for Ergu—a lovely green lantern shaped like a rabbit. And as for Little Pear—well! He had had a trip to the fair!

9

Little Pear Falls into the River and Decides to Be Good

It was a hot day in the middle of the summer. The sun blazed down on the village and on Little Pear, who was strolling along the street, eating a cucumber. His bare feet shuffled through the thick yellow dust. "Ay-ah," he sighed, "how hot it is!— and where are all my friends?"

The street was deserted, and the reason was that nearly everyone was asleep. It was too hot for most people to want to walk about. It was even too hot for the children to want to play. Little Pear, though, always wanted to be doing something. "I know what I shall do," he thought. "I shall go and watch the boats on the river." Just then he saw a child trotting around the corner. He felt quite excited for a minute, because he had walked nearly through half the village and had seen only a pig and a few chickens. But when the child came nearer he saw that it was only Big Head's baby brother.

The baby was dressed in a little red apron shaped

like a diamond. It was all that he had on, because Chinese babies don't wear very much in the summer. His head was shaved except for a fringe of hair across his forehead. He was trotting along in a great hurry until he met Little Pear, who stopped him. "You must not run away," said Little Pear, and he took the baby's hand and led him back to the home of Big Head, who was leaning against the doorway, fast asleep. Little Pear lifted the little brother over the

doorstep and gave him the rest of his cucumber. "Stay where you are," he said. "You might get lost if you run away." Then he had a good idea. He took the good-luck chain off his own neck and put it around the baby's. "Now you will be safe," he said, and he patted the baby kindly on the head and strolled on, feeling very good. Again he thought, "I shall go to the river and watch the ships," and he started off in the direction of the river.

It was a long way to the river. Little Pear followed the path that cut across the fields, and soon left the village far behind him. The sun blazed down on Little Pear as he pattered along in his bare feet. The

He soon left the village far behind

fields were as deserted as the village. There was no sound except for the singing of cicadas in the willow trees as he drew near the river.

Presently he stood on the high bank, looking down at the river. First he looked up the river, and then he looked down the river; and all the time he remembered to hold tight to a willow tree with both hands.

The river was swift and muddy. The sun shining on it made the ripples first brown and then blue. The bank opposite Little Pear, like the bank that he was standing on, was bordered by rough-barked willow trees leaning out over the water. Between the banks the boats went busily up and down. Here everybody seemed to be very wide awake. Little Pear thought of the sleepy village he had left and was glad that he had come to the river.

There were all kinds of boats. Big boats with masts and sails and smaller boats with none, and boats with great fishing nets spread out like huge spiderwebs. There were flat boats, too, laden with things to sell. Some had cabbages, and some had rolls of matting, and some had bags that might be filled with all sorts of interesting things, Little Pear thought.

The big boats had eyes painted on them in front, so that they could see where they were going. The

owners of these boats were careful not to let anything
hang over the edge in front of the eyes, for then the
boats could not have seen their way as they sailed
in and out among the smaller boats.

Little Pear wished that he had a boat of his own,
but he couldn't decide whether he would rather have
a small one that he could row, or a larger one that
he could push with a pole, or a *big* one with a sail.

Finally Little Pear decided that what he would
like most of all to have when he grew up would be
a fishing boat. For then he could catch fish for his

He held tight to the willow tree

meals and take fish to the city to sell, and what fun
that would be!

Little Pear held tight to the willow tree and gazed
at the ships going up and down. He was wishing
that he would grow up soon, when suddenly he saw,
drawing nearer and nearer, the loveliest kind of boat
on the river. It was a houseboat!

"That is the kind of boat I should like to have,"
thought Little Pear as he watched it drawing nearer
and nearer. It was a long flat boat with a real little
house on it, with a hole in the ceiling for the smoke
to go through, and paper windows. A man was walk-
ing up and down the side of the deck, shoving with
a long pole.

Little Pear looked admiringly at the clothes
hanging out to dry and watched the children playing

about the deck, and the boat sailed gaily along until it was quite close to Little Pear.

Suddenly, one of the children saw him. He called to his brothers and sisters, and they all flocked to the edge of the boat and waved to Little Pear as he stood alone on the bank. It made him feel very happy, and without thinking he let go of his tree to wave back. *Slip,* went his feet on the steep bank— slip, slide—and *plop,* into the river fell Little Pear! . . .

The brown water whirled round and round him

in circles as he rose to the surface, choking and sputtering. "Ay-ah!" cried the children on the boat. "He is drowning, he is drowning!" For Little Pear could not swim, and the swift current was carrying him away from the bank. He splashed around wildly with his arms and was about to sink again when the man on the boat rushed forward and reached out his pole. "Catch hold!" he cried.

Little Pear couldn't hear what the man said, for there was water in his ears. He could scarcely see the man, for there was water in his eyes! He couldn't say anything himself, for he had swallowed so much water—but he splashed around with his arms—and—he caught hold of the pole! Then he held on tight while the man pulled him to the side of the boat and lifted him safely to the deck.

For some time he lay there, wondering to himself whether he was drowned or not, and thinking that perhaps he would never see his family again. Then he opened his eyes and saw above him a circle of

faces. Here he was on the houseboat, and here were the children who had waved to him and the man who had saved him. There was the kindly face of the mother, too, who had hurried out of the little house to see what had happened.

Little Pear smiled at them, and they all exclaimed over him, saying what a wonder it was that he wasn't drowned; and they admired his flowered jacket and the green string around his pigtail.

"Will you stay with us?" asked the children.

But their mother said, "No, this little boy comes from the shore, and his family will wonder where he is. He must go home when we come to the next landing-place."

The boat sailed on down the river. Little Pear sat drying in the sun, while the children sat around him in a circle, telling him about their life on the river, and asking him eager questions about the land. "We have never lived on the land," they told

him, "because this boat has always been our home."
Then Little Pear told them about his village, and
about his family and friends and his canary. As he
talked he began to think how glad he would be to
see them all again. But the boat sailed on down the
busy river, taking Little Pear farther and farther
away from home.

When they finally reached the next landing-place,

the houseboat stopped and Little Pear was set ashore.
He felt very sorry to say good-bye to his new friends.
He climbed the path up the bank and watched until
the boat had sailed on, far down the river. The
children were still waving to him, but Little Pear
held tight to a tree with both hands, because he
didn't want to fall into the water again. The boat
disappeared around a bend in the river, and Little
Pear started for home.

Away across the fields the sun was setting. Little Pear walked on, and on, and on. The way home was long, as the boat had sailed a mile or two down the river. "Ay-ah," thought Little Pear, "soon it will be dark!" And he hurried his tired feet along more quickly. He wished that he might meet another kind man like his friend who had taken him to the city. But the path along the river bank was deserted, the fields were deserted, and it seemed as though in all the world there was nobody except Little Pear.

Little Pear walked on, and on, and on. The sun had been down for a long time, and the night was very dark, when at last Little Pear saw ahead of him the dim outline of the village. Dogs barked at him as he approached. "Don't bark!" he cried. "Don't you know me? This is Little Pear!" When he reached his own gateway the stone lions on either side of it looked very fierce. "They are roaring now, not laughing," he thought, and he said aloud, "Don't bite me. This is Little Pear!" He ran across the courtyard to the house. "Open the door!" he cried. "It is Little Pear!"

Then the door was flung open, and "It is Little Pear!" cried his mother and Dagu and Ergu all at once, throwing their arms around him.

How glad Little Pear was to be at home again! And how glad his family was to see him! "Where

have you been?" they cried. "We have hunted for you all afternoon, and the men are still out with lanterns, looking for you."

Little Pear told them all that had happened, how he had left the village and had gone to the river, and how he had fallen into the river and been rescued. Then his mother prepared some hot food for him while Dagu put the kettle on to boil and Ergu sped away to tell all the village that Little Pear had returned.

Soon there was the sound of many feet in the courtyard, and then the tiny room was filled with people. There were Little Pear's father and the other men who had been searching with him for Little Pear. There was Ergu, out of breath and with shining eyes. There were all the nearest neighbors and best friends. There was Big Head, looking very excited, and Big Head's baby brother, eating a tang-hulur. He still had the good-luck chain around his neck.

"You may keep the chain," Little Pear told him, "for you are very little and something might happen to you. But I am a big boy, and I am never going to run away again."

Then everybody was very happy. They patted

"I am never going to run away again"

Little Pear on the head, and the baby brother gave him the rest of his tang-hulur.

"We all loved you very much when you were naughty," they said, "but we shall love you even more if you are good."

"I will always be a good boy now," Little Pear promised, nodding his head very hard. Ergu looked at her small brother and suddenly felt rather sad.

"Little Pear is growing up," she said.